LATEST EDITION

THE SECRET OF
HIS BOUNTY

The Story of a Homeless Man?
You Decide

Donielle Ingersoll

ISBN Paperback 978-1-965126-03-5
ISBN Hardback 978-1-965126-04-2
ISBN eBook   978-1-965126-05-9

Printed in the United States of America.

www.eastwenatcheepublishing.com

Contents

PROLOGUE

Chinese Proverb: Tell me, I forget. Show me, I remember. Involve me, I understand and act.

Deep in the Himalayan Mountains' heart is an enchanted kingdom of near immortals. They have existed there for thousands of years. Few humans have ever been to this empire. If any of our kind ever entered, it was by invitation only and probably because they were exceptional. Take the King, Elvis Presley, for instance. You would have to admit that he was quite exceptional. Perhaps he is an example of a human who, by invitation alone, would have been escorted to this land of forever or one of many of its kind, stationed around our globe. What exceptional humans can you think of who perhaps died of questionable circumstances? Leonardo da Vinci? He was centuries ahead of his time, as were people like Tesla and our great philosophers who changed the world. Then, there is the entire realm of religion. What about the greats like Buddha, Confucius, Mohammed, and Jesus? We are talking about really exceptional people here. Perhaps some of these very ones got an invitation to a secluded paradise. It would be a one-way ticket for most, for once you enter this place of enlightenment, few ever return, that is, if you are human. Not the ancient gods, though; they can come and go at will. Take a look at Greek, Egyptian, and Chinese Mythology. There are many of these ancient gods who reside in this land of immortals or use it as a stop-off point between their interstellar trips. Also, some who would visit there could include the Anunnaki with their fabled planet that comes close to Earth every three millennia or so, and the eagle-headed humans so often seen in hieroglyphs.

Many of the great men of Earth heard of this land of wonder and sent expeditions to find it. There was Alexander the Great, Napoleon, and Hitler, to name a few. If they could only find it and seek entrance, there were vast secrets to be known. There is the hint of some remnant of Eden inside, almost as if the tree of life itself is within, yet we know that is not possible. Life expectancy in this place is miraculous, to say the least. Were one to die at age 300, they would be but a youth. If your body became old, they would clone a new, younger you and transfer your mind from the old to the new. There are medicines there that would cure any disease known to man. And the technological wonders? I could fill pages and pages with them, one after another. You have never seen architecture such as you would see in this exotic place. There are substances not known to exist on Earth that are common there; many have been transported from galaxies beyond our present reach. I personally have never been to this place, but I have seen portions of it out on the fringes of my mind, hanging there like a mirage. I could spend weeks talking about its beauty. Ah, to get lost in its expanse! I would be gone for months, just roaming, seeing, living, and experiencing it, taking in all its amazing wonders. James Hilton hardly scratched the surface, for within the mountain of Karakal is a vast underground civilization. The ascending lamas, with their civilization of around one thousand, are just a front covering one to the three entrances to the empire. Only the highest members of the order know this. That is not to say they are the immortals; they are not, though living so close to such longevity lengthens their age up to and past a couple of centuries if they are fortunate.

Perhaps some of the oldest and most acclaimed

members of the lamasery have been granted entrance to the mountain if they, during their short stay on Earth, attained the right mindset. Yes, over the centuries, there have been some who have been admitted though few. When these master lamas were well advanced in the human aging process and about to pass from this world, some of them attained the mental state necessary to penetrate the barrier. This occurred either by chance or design; no one will ever tell you. Once within the mountain, they grew increasingly younger rather than older. Their aging process was reversed, and the vigor of youth returned while their mind still maintained its mental age. Perhaps after five centuries had passed, some were granted permission to mingle with civilization again since, by that time, all attachment to earthly things had perished. Presently, the oldest members of this advanced order may do studies that require them to enter society again. It all depends on the individual circumstances and whether or not it would be beneficial for the whole. This inner civilization has been one of the best-kept secrets in the world. If I were to tell you more of its secret mysteries, woe be unto me, for some of those mysteries must never be printed on pages of white.

What are humans to these near immortals? We are but cattle; they breed us and herd us around like sheep in a pasture. We are their slaves if the truth were known. Many there consider us a scourge on the planet. They would wipe us out of existence and have indeed done that in ages past. Entire civilizations have been eliminated with little traces that would show they ever existed. There would be much more death among us from them, but there is a balancing intelligence in the universe that will only allow them to go so far and no further. So, we live on here, going about our daily lives as if we are the only ones that matter. We get caught up in so much of nothing, squabbling and scrapping over trinkets: self-exultation is our god. So why am I starting this story in this particular manner? Does it have anything to do with homelessness in America and the story of one homeless man? Perhaps it does, perhaps it does not? Would you like to take a trip into this enchanted kingdom of wonders beyond imagination, this kingdom of immortals? What if you knew that once you gained entrance, you, too, would become immortal? If you were an immortal, what would you do with all the time on your hands? Do immortals have boring days, weeks, months, or years? Perhaps this is the substance for another story, perhaps not?

CHAPTER 1

Chinese Proverb: Habits are cobwebs at first, cables at last.

Philami rattled into camp around 9.00 am on a Friday morning. The Ford truck was old and smashed up in places. There was a taillight and headlight out. The license plate tag was the same color as the current ones on the road, but a closer look would show it to be 6 years expired. To look at the rig one might call it a rust bucket. There were some things in the back, boxes, and bundles, that did not look promising. He seemed to know where to go. There was one place where a bunch of garbage had been piled. From the outside it looked bad but by moving a few things, the bearded oriental had a place to drive the truck off the road in no time. The residents were surprised. They had marked out their territories with their own code of ethics. Each knew of these invisible boundaries. The funny thing of it was where Phil cleared things away, no one had claimed that territory. It was wide open. All he had to do was pile up some of the scattered garbage and discarded items that had been tossed there. As he did this, some nasty smelling odors became air born along with a gaggle of flies and wasps. None of it seemed to bother the newcomer. He set to work and had things looking pretty good in short order. By this time residents of the camp from all sides had moseyed over to have a look. It was clear that he was headed for old Reggie's tent. The residents had not seen him out and about for a couple of days but that was normal for the old drunk. A person had to be really hammered to be called an old drunk in a place like this. Yup. That was Reggie for you. Once he got ahold of some of that hard stuff he stayed out of sight for hours, sometimes days. Finally, the destination was reached. He opened the tent flap and went in. In a couple of minutes later he was back out doing something with some sort of pager.

Half an hour later, a late model SUV showed up. A middle-aged woman was behind the wheel. She waited for Philami to arrive before opening the door. She was not about to take any chances in a place like this. About as soon as she opened the door, she closed it again and fiddled around for a mask. Though the bearded man had no problem with the air quality it was apparent this woman had a lot of problems with it. With the mask fully in place she opened the door again and got out. With a click of her hand the rig was locked up as she followed him to the tent. They entered. About five minutes later they emerged.

"So, it was your father, Matty," the man questioned as they headed back to the car.

"Yes, that is him. He dropped out of our lives a dozen years or so ago, refused to have anything to do with any of us. We tried to keep in communication with him, but he moved around a lot. I had no idea he had sunk this low. Why? He was making over $200,000.00 a year as CO of TecKraft. I do not understand?" Matty unlocked the door to her vehicle and got inside. Was that a tear creeping down her cheek? If it was, it was absorbed by the mask.

"To answer your question, it is hard to say why people do what they do. It is all about the little choices they make in life. After a time, those little choices become bigger and bigger, but the individuals hardly notice the change. It just grows and grows. If you were to see him one week and then come back a month later, you would see a big difference but not people like your father. He could not see himself changing at all. What do you plan to do?" The new man in town rubbed his snowy white beard as he looked into her eyes. They were staring out at him above the mask and below her hairline.

"I have called M&M Funeral Home. They will be here in a few minutes to take him to their parlor. He will be fixed up I suppose as best they can. It looks like he has been dead for at least two days if not longer. He had a lot of friends in his day. Some were very influential. Mom wanted to do it up right. Deep down inside she really loved him. It is just that he became impossible to live with after a while. Once he was home, he would drink nonstop. I can't remember seeing him without a glass in his hand during the last few weeks before he left." The SUV drove off and just as she stated, a hurst arrived about 15 minutes later. Phil showed them to the tent, and they removed him after putting him in a black bag and zipping it shut. Thus ended the reign of Reggie Harold Minesinger.

After he was gone, Phil cleaned up around his camp.

It was bad, really bad. There were feces all over the place mingled with old rags and rotten toilet paper. The addict had tossed lots of bottles off to the side once he was finished downing their contents. Many had broken and glass was scattered all over the ground. Hoards of flies were swarming the encampment. Philami shoveled all of it up and put it in bags then piled them off to the side. The lady had been bombarded with the flies but not the oriental. He seemed to take no mind of the smell and mess. But then if he was a true homeless person, his senses had most likely adapted to it as part of life. Once the old man's tent was down and the junk cleaned away, this stranger brought out a bag of lime and sprinkled it all over. He had formed a perfect square. It did not look like it was even an inch off from any angle. At each corner he drove an anchoring rod about two feet into the ground. Next, he put up his old, camouflage tent. There were a couple of holes in the back, but he did not seem to mind. At this time of year, it didn't rain much anyway. Next, he made a ring of rocks not far from the entrance. This would be his fire pit. At last, he took the bundles and boxes out of the back of the pickup and stashed them inside. He was home.

In his tent, Phil had a cot, a table and two chairs. There were a couple of crates tipped up on end to form supports for a board. Once placed on top, it made a pretty good shelf. He had a lamp that appeared to burn without any fuel. It was quite amazing like the Tesla fire starter. It worked but you didn't know how. There was also a little heater that could hook up to an electrical outlet if this place had one. It did not, at least not today. This would be one of his first projects, to get power. Any places that had power were claimed long before Philami came into town. He had brought staples with him also. Perhaps he had gone shopping at a grocery store, who knows? It had taken him most of the day to do all this. About dusk he started a fire in the pit and put a pot of water on to boil. Soon he had a savory stew cooking over the open flames. Once it was hot, he did an amazing thing. He dished up exactly 7 bowels and placed 6 just outside of his square on an old table he had rescued from the junk. It had a missing leg, so he propped that end of the table up with an old bucket and some broken bricks. Thus started the amazing adventures of this unusual homeless person. Over the next several weeks the entire camp would change. The ways and means of this remarkable feat is portrayed hereafter.

CHAPTER 2

Chinese Proverb: A journey of a thousand miles begins with a single step.

News traveled fast among the residents of this homeless camp. It was located in one of the larger metropolises, almost perfectly centered between the east and west coast. The Mutt and Jeff of this shanty town heard of the newcomer and hatched a plan between them. He had a truck. It didn't matter if it was purdy or not, it was worth its weight in the services it could provide. They were kind of the head honchos in this place and did not take kindly to newcomers. They would kill him, make it look like an accident and claim his treasures for their own. The event would go down shortly after midnight. When the hour arrived, they crept into his camp. Immediately there was a high-pitched sound that penetrated their ear drums. The closer they got to the tent the more painful it became. By the time they were ten yards away they could stand it no longer, so they crept back and went around to check out the truck. As they approached it, there was a different sound that penetrated their ears. This one was so deep it rattled their skulls. Their teeth started to vibrate, knocking together with a distinct buzzing sound. If they had gone any closer, the 13 teeth they shared between them might have rattled right out of their jaws. Mutt and Jeff never returned to bother him again. Others who tried to invade his space met with the same fate. If Phil knew of this, he didn't show it. He acted as if everything was perfectly normal.

The stew he had made the night before disappeared from the table quickly. Nine people went to bed with something besides booze in their bellies. The next morning the ritual was repeated. This time oatmeal was on the menu along with some bananas and orange juice. Again, there were 6 bowls set out on the old table along with as many bananas and paper cups filled with OJ. It was a meal that many in the world today would despise but to some hungry, homeless people, it was wonderful! After eating, Philami went to 5 scrap piles not far from his tent and brought an assortment of items back. There was a toaster, a propeller from an old boat, an engine from an old mower and a few other things. He set to work and soon had what appeared to be a motorized propeller thing-a-ma-giggy. He was having trouble putting it together exactly like he wanted. He spent 5 hours without success. John was watching from three tents over. Something started to stir in his benumbed mind. Back in civilization, John had been an engineer. He even had a couple of his inventions patented. He came over to the edge and was looking on with interest. Phil noticed and spoke to him.

"You are John, right? The man nodded before he responded.

"Yes. I was noticing you were trying hard to make something. Is it a wind generator?"

"You are very insightful, John. How did you figure it out?" The older man shrugged his shoulders with a sense of non-interest before answering. "You added a generator. I guess that is what gave it away. I think if you switched the polarity inside, when the wind blows the propellers, it will put out voltage. I see you also scrounged up half a dozen old batteries. Let me get something that will bring them a little life." John left Phil's camp and returned a few minutes later with a yellow liquid. He took the old screw driver Philami was using and opened all the caps. If the liquid was down, he poured some of the yellow stuff in to bring them up to level. It was foul smelling. Where Phil had not been bothered by other rotten smells all over the place, this stuff caused him to wrinkle up his nose and partially cover it with his upper lip. Soon all were ready. John hooked up some cables to the unit and connected them to the battery array. Then he connected an outlet to the contraption. There was an old, rusted iron with a cord not far away. This he plugged into the outlet. A sharp wind had come up and the propellers were moving. In a few minutes, the engineer wet his finger tip and touched the iron. He was rewarded with a hissing sound and a slight burn. John was very pleased. He showed it all over.

From the back of his truck, Phil brought out an old electrical harness from some vehicle and made a few more connections. He brought four units out of his tent that looked like they came from another planet then went to each corner of his plot. He mounted a unit on each anchoring rod he had sunk into the ground the day before. After that was done, he activated each one starting at the north east corner. There was a little switch that he flipped on. When the last switch was activated, a blue arch of something came from each unit making what looked to be a laser. John looked on with wonder. In no time besides the power on a pole there was also power to each unit he had mounted. The makeshift wind turbine seemed to turn even faster. Phil knew that even if the wind stopped, the propellers would still turn, and the power never go off. John did not know that though. He would never tell him either. He turned to the visitor in his camp and complemented him before asking a question.

"You are amazing, John. What are you doing here? You could be putting those skills to work for you. You could have a nice place and a decent life." John hung his head a little before responding. He too had a beard nearly as long as the oriental's but instead of white his was a mixture of gray and white.

"They fired me. I was doing good until then. Got a little woman and a couple of kids back in the country. I tried to find work but the guy I worked for was influential and told me I would never work in this town again and he has been right on. Word about his displeasure with me always got there before I did, and they never gave me a chance." Phil thought about this for awhile before going into his tent. He came out with another of the contraptions he had mounted on the rods. He explained how it worked and what it did, then he made an offer.

"You probably understand the principle behind this gadget better than I do, right?" He watched the expression of the man before continuing. "If you can put out 10 of these a day, you can make a decent living. I can sell as many of these as can be produced for a decent price. If you have your own manufacturing business, nobody can fire you, can they? Old John got a real spark of interest in his eyes this time. He was thinking it over.

"Do you think Nancy would take me back after all of this time?" Phil thought hard and long before answering.

"Do you love her?"

"Yes, very much. I don't know if she loves me anymore though. She got pretty mad when we lost the house because we couldn't make the mortgage payments."

"I will tell you what, John. You make up a few of these and come back by with them. I will pay you then. After a week you should try to contact her and see if she is still interested in a relationship with you. How long has it been since you have seen your grandchildren?"

"How did you know I had grandkids?" Philami was silent for a minute before doing something so unusual,

John was amazed.

"There names are Jenny and David, aren't they?" This time John was really surprised. He started to shake a little. He was having a withdrawal from being off his needle for so long. "You need a fix don't you. And you feel if you have not overcome your addiction, she will never take you back. You are right. But I can help." Phil went into his tent and came out with a shovel. He proceeded to the edge of a pile of junk and tugged on a tall weed. With a few strokes of the shovel, he had it out roots and all. They were long and yellow. He stoked the fire and put the pot on to boil. Before it ever started, he took the roots over to one of the blue laser beams, placed a bowl underneath and run the roots through it. Every time he brought the root down a little piece of it was cut off and dropped into the bowl. It was slicker than any knife John had ever seen. Philami knew that probably 50 pair of eyes were peering at them from behind the piles of junk. That was what was supposed to happen. He wanted to make a point to them. Ten minutes later he gave old John a paper cup filled with the hot liquid. The druggy smelled it. It was not a good smell. "It will not taste like a cream soda." John was again amazed for his favorite soda had been orange cream. "But if you really value a relationship with Nancy, you will do this for her, and yourself." With that encouragement the man started to drink it. Phil led him over to his only other chair and bid him sit down. In a few minutes, his trembling hand stopped shaking. It was a miracle. The old craving was simply not there. "You will need to drink this once in the morning and once at night for the next week while you are working on the units. The only way you will go back to the needle is if you deliberately choose to do so. You will not feel a need for it again." Philami dipped enough juice out of the kettle to fill 6 paper cups and placed them on the old table just beyond the blue beams.

There was something amazing happening also. So long as you had an invitation to interact with Phil, no agonizing vibration pulverized your ear drums. The bearded oriental handed John a box of parts after he had finished the last drop from the cup. He pulled out his pager-if that was what it really was-and pushed the button. The blue beams disappeared from all sides of his camp. John walked away with the box under his arm. Phil looked over at the table. All six cups had disappeared. Deep inside he was happy. He would faithfully place six cups out every morning and evening when John came by. Perhaps there would be fewer addicts on the street come a week from now.

CHAPTER 3

Chinese Proverb: A crisis is an opportunity riding on dangerous winds.

The next morning after giving John another cup of the weed root tea and frying up some eggs, bacon, and pancakes for 5 other people out there, he headed off to town in the old truck. It was not a very good part of town. There were many unsavory characters mulling around. The Chinese man placed all his senses on high alert as he walked among them to a thrift store with bars over the windows and doors. He was about to enter when he saw a man rush out and grab a woman from behind. He wrestled her to the ground and while pinning her hands down with one arm and her legs with his knee started to tug at her pants. He was going to rape her there in broad daylight. Philami looked on with amazement! Was no one going to do anything? At least a dozen people were within reach of them. Most did not even pay her screams of protest any mind. Something came over him, something he had not felt in a very long time. With amazing agility, the oriental man struck with lightning swift kicks. In a matter of seconds, the big guy was crunched unconscious under a metal bench that was bolted to the sidewalk. He gave him one more well positioned strike, one that would render him unconscious for another 20 minutes at least before going over to the woman. She had gained her footing and had her pants back up when he approached. A stream of foul words came from her mouth. She cussed him up one side and down the other. If he had been amazed before, this was even more so. Coming right up to his face she spat in it and turned to go still muttering foul words under her breath.

Philami started to chant one of his poems. Back in his day he was known for his renown poetry. The sound that came from his abdomen up through his throat was mournful like the distant whaling of a coyote or a deep throated owl. It rose in pitch to a high level then vibrated like an oscillator as he brought the scale back down lower and lower. All the people within 100 feet around were paralyzed by it. They stood still as if frozen in time and so they were. Phil could have gone up to any one of them and picked their pocket and none would have noticed. He put his two hands together and made another unusual sound and all the people came out of their trance. Then something very strange happened. The people on the street had never seen such a thing. After cussing him out and spitting in his face the woman returned and knelt in front of him. From those same lips came words of apology and remorse.

"I am so sorry for what I did to you. Can you ever forgive me? Something comes over me at times like this and I lose all control. Whatever you did, that sound you made caused that thing that has been bothering me for 2 years to depart. When it came, I had no power to resist. It took possession of me and I did terrible things. I was a respected woman once with a nice career. I had a husband that I deeply loved. Then I started playing around with dark things. It was alluring at first. But as it gained more power over me, it forced me to do terrible things. I became a woman of the night, sleeping with men, several far worse than that fellow there under the bench. Such horrible things. It was a nightmare. But you, you did something."

Phil had listened to her speech as she prostrated herself before him. Empathy came over him for this woman. Back in his mind he followed the voice of intuition that never failed to lead him in the right direction no matter what the circumstances. Then he responded. "Jack says to tell you these two words. I do not know what they mean unless they refer to a certain song that made its way to the top of your charts several years ago. Does "Yellow Ribbon," mean anything to you?" The lady reached out and grasp his feet and started to cry. Then through tear filled eyes responded.

"Did Jack really tell you to say those words, 'Yellow ribbon?"

"He did indeed. Why? What is it all about?

"He still loves me after all that I have done. He still wants me to come back to him. We had such a wonderful life together. I think he would be considered my soulmate if the truth were known. If Jack wants me back and this thing has gone from me, I will clean myself up. I will buy the nicest dress I can find. I will wear his favorite perfume and I will go back to him. You saved my life. How can I ever thank you?" Phil pulled two one-hundred-dollar bills from his pocket and handed them to the grateful woman.

"Use these to make yourself presentable. And may you, Janice and your love, Jack live a long and prosperous life. I see two lovely children in the near future for you. Do not betray the trust I have placed in you, do you understand?" Janice got up from the ground, placed her arms around the surprised oriental man and gave him a sweet kiss on his cheek.

"As God is my witness, I am a changed woman. Thank you for a second chance to the life of my dreams. I believe that dream will come true, and the children-Jack always wanted me to give him-will come just as you prophesied. We will do it and raise them to be respectable citizens. Thank you again." With that she was gone. Philami retraced his steps to the store and went in to purchase the items he needed. After the fourth trip they were loaded into the back of his truck. On his last trip out, he saw the man under the bench stirring so went over and gave him another blow that put him back into never, never land. When he woke up the next time, he would remember none of what had happened neither would any of the people that had witnessed this strange occurrence, not even Janice. In every one of their lives good changes would come. Even the man under the bench would make something of himself besides a street thug. The ancient song would go to work within them unnoticed as they started their new lives.

Back in camp he hooked up the small refrigerator to one of the power sources at one corner of his camp. He placed a heat coil in a large tank he had secured from the store and drove a pipe with a spicket on it about 3 feet into the ground. Once the pipe was secured, he entered his tent and opened an old case that looked as if it should have been in one of the junk piles. This however, contained his most cherished treasure. It held a two-edged ancient sword. Typically, one would expect it to be sharp, but this was not the case. It was surprisingly dull. Made of a silvery metal it was well tarnished. Removing it carefully, he took it over to the pipe and pushed it into the ground on the left. Then he chanted another one of his many poems. It was a bit different than the song he had done earlier. The sword had the power to cause him and any activity to he did to be invisible. The people watching from behind the piles of junk and shrubbery, must never remember this ritual. The chant would erase any memory of it. After finishing, while the observers were still in a trance, he returned the sword to its case, then closed and locked it. It was then returned to its place under his cot. Coming back out to the pipe he uttered two words before proceeding to hook an old hose also from the same store to the faucet. Much to the amazement of all the onlookers, when he turned the handle, pure, fresh, clean water came pouring out of the end of the hose. He placed it in the tank and soon had it filled up. He plugged the cord to the heating coil into another corner power source. Then driving 4 galvanized pipes into the ground he surrounded them with a tarp he had also purchased. Tonight, after supper he would take a nice, long hot shower. It would be right after John came to drink his tea. This would be a wonderful change. After being grimy from all the nasty stuff he had moved, he could wash it all away. It would be heavenly to feel that warm liquid cleanse his filthy body. Once everything was out of his truck and John had presented him with 5 units all completed, he activated the laser system around his camp and headed for the shower room. Tomorrow he would install a toilet.

CHAPTER 4

Chinese Proverb: Solve one problem and you keep a hundred others away.

As the sun tried to rise over the smoggy city horizon, Philami woke up quite contented. The hot shower had relaxed him. It was so good to be clean after living in the grime for a few days. He opened the little leather pouch and checked his talisman by placing it up to his temple. He could feel the energy radiating from it, but it would need to be re-energized the next time the full moon came into the heavens. That might mean a trip out of the city. It had enough power to do what needed to be done today. However, this process would drain it more than he liked. Back in the ancient days an alchemist had crafted it from his own life force. There was a process by which you captured it and refined it, then processed it into a solid form. At one step silver dust needed to be added to ferment it. It was a soft stone of a rippled green color almost the color and consistency of soapstone. If he found himself feeling a bit drained or tired, all he had to do was take his golden pocket knife out and scrape a little of the substance off into a cup. Any liquid could be added then. It would soak for about an hour and then be sipped like you would do if you were having tea. People had been known to be sustained from starvation with this elixir for weeks if they were imprisoned. The only other element they needed was water. That was also available from a small unit the Chinese man had in his tent. Every day there would be the six extra cups of yellowroot set out for the homeless after John left. He had made a little extra this morning. The remaining cup was sitting on a stand over by his faucet. He scrapped a little powder off the stone and returned it to its leather pouch after stirring it into the liquid.

It was strange how the substance of the stone worked. It had an entirely different approach to healing than medicine had. It worked from a molecular approach to healing, reviving the electrical energy in the cells of the body. There was a magnetic property about it that charged up the protons and electrons that made up the physical structure of the cells themselves. Fully vitalized by this, the organs were free to cast off toxins that had been trapped in them and undergo beta cell regeneration. The stone existed in two dimensions at one time. It was part of the fourth as well as the third dimension. It would connect the body to the fourth dimension by means of this electrical property. There were little cells in the body that responded to light energy. They would get clogged up with all the junk people put in their belly. Once scrubbed clean, these cells could vitalize the entire electrical forces of the person. Philami had seen it work miracles. People that were nearly dead had been brought back from the very edge and made full recoveries in a matter of days once these electrical forces in their body had been realigned. This process using molecular medicine rather than drugs was all outlined in some of the ancient Chinese medical manuscripts he had access to from his many years in Shangri-La. John brought over another five units. If the laser beam were visible, he would signal Phil to turn it off so he could enter the camp. He was all smiles this morning.

"Dr. Phil! That foul tasting tea you have been making for me is amazing! This is my third day without any craving for that white powder. A resident was sniffing some when I went by and it almost caused me to throw up. You are a miracle worker! The ancient sage pondered his remarks for a few seconds before responding.

"When you relieve yourself, what color is your urine?"

"I meant to talk with you about that. It is deep yellow almost orange. And when it comes out it burns a bit. Is that normal?"

"You need to drink at least three quarts of water. The elixir is purging your body of all the toxins that have been building up in your cells. You need to flush them out of your system. I saw several whisky bottles around. Find one of the larger ones with a cap. Take it over to the spicket and use that dish soap to clean it out real good. Then fill it up with water. Drink that much at least every day. If you are still dark yellow, increase it by a couple of glasses until it is light yellow or white."

"I really never developed a taste for water," the old engineer responded as he looked over at a pile of junk just outside of Phil's camp. He spotted a bottle that was light green and of a pop-bellied shape. The lid was rusty so he saw a shiny one that looked like it would fit and tried it out. It was a match. A foul smell came out of the green bottle as he opened it up. In short order by the sink however, it was a lot better. He filled it full and took a big swig.

"I have one thing to say for water. Even though I do not like the taste of water, it sure beats the taste of that nasty yellowroot. So, I am going to enjoy this." With that he left the camp. Philami pushed the button. There was a buzzing sound and the laser activated again. He looked at the five units the man had put together and then checked them out. He had a special activation key that slipped into a small slot. This he would turn and if good, the units would give off two beeps. Every one of them performed top notch. John had told him to hold unto the money until he was ready to leave, then give it to him all at once. Philami promised to pay him in gold coins. These he could take down to the exchanger and get good money for.

Phil next went over to the spot where his toilet would be placed. At the second-hand store he had found one that would work. There was one problem with it so far as he was concerned. It was pink. I suppose the old saying is true. "Beggars can't be choosers." Phil had a little unit in his pocket that allowed him to pass through the beam without being cut off at the legs. He went to the truck and pulled out some old crates he had picked up from the back of the thrift store. These he arranged in a square around the toilet. He attached a plastic hose to plumb it. There was one thing this camp had that helped a great deal. There was a sewer channel running directly under the far side of the camp. He could just catch a few inches of it. He connected the toilet to an assortment of pips he had scrounged up and in about an hour, had a working toilet with his own septic outlet. Now it was time to go on the mission he had planned ever since entering the area.

A very pitiful black man with diabetes was camped about five junk piles over. He could barely get out of his shack. He did not even have a tent. He had stretched out some wood pallets and placed cardboard on the inside to keep out a little of the cold. He had found an old cot with the legs gone on one side but had set up some broken bricks so it would hold his weight. He was large. His spot was not far from a dumpster where a market threw out all its really old breads and sweets. There were also some half rotten fruit or vegetables that ended up in there also. He had a streetwise son who came and fished the stuff out for him every couple of days so Abel would not have to go very far. He could hardly walk. The neuropathy in his legs and feet were so bad he could feel nothing but pain. As he chanced to pass a couple of days earlier, Phil noticed some of his toes had been chewed on by rats. That was a big problem in this homeless camp. There were hundreds of them. They climbed over everything and were into everything. At night if you shown a flashlight around their little beady eyes would show before they scrambled off. You knew it was really bad when some of the eyes looking back in your direction showed red in the light.

Phil took one of the units John had made. Opened it up and then going to a locked box, opened it up and took out a circuit board. It had a place where one could connect it to the inside of the box. This he did. Once closed again and activated, it put out a high-pitched sound that drove rats crazy. It got inside their brains and literally set off vibrations that turned them to jelly. The rats ended up dying in a great deal of pain. The only problem was with the distance of transmission. It only worked in a thirty-foot diameter from the transmission source. Philami had found an old radio in the thrift store with an amplifier. He figured out there was enough room inside if he run a jumper wire over to it. With the modifications made, he figured it would about double the area of transmission. Now he was ready. He took his leave.

Abel was sleeping as the Oriental Man entered his camp. He made a little noise to rouse him. He felt sure by now news had spread to him of the newcomer.

"How are you doing today, Abel." Phil ask in a rather loud voice. "I am here to see if there is something that can be done about all of the rats. Are you awake?"

"Yah I'm awake now wha deh ya say bout rats? I'z kinda hard o herein."

"I am Phil, your neighbor and have come to get the rats out of the area around your pad. I have a little device that will keep them away for good. You will not even know it is activated. It goes to work and paralyzes them so they can't move and die in a few minutes."

"Don't know nuttin bout dat, good sir. But if you wan som dem rats, take all you care. Good riddance I say." Phil showed his face for the first time to the old man. He remarked. "Whaa day say bout yaz'all be de truth den. I seed it wid deez ol eyes meself. Youze shaw is a China man threw an threw. I never seed such slanted eyes as dem China uns. You lookie jus like um." Hee, Hee." Phil did not respond negatively to the remark at all. He placed the unit down and slid it into a blank place at the bottom of the cot. This tent reeked with the smell of urine and refuse. Most anyone would have heaved up all the food they had eaten in the last 24 hours, but this Oriental was well trained after years and years. He could block out things in his senses. He could nearly levitate so rather than walk into camp, he had enough control of the elements to bounce slightly and glide, every now and then he would put a toe or heel down to steer to the left or right. This way he could kinda skim over the surface of the ground without maximum contact with all the filth.

"I want to give you something that will help with your nerve pain down in those legs of yours. I notice they are really swollen also. Your legs are retaining water. That means your heart has a lot of water around it too. You are a heart attack waiting to happen. Will you let me help you with that pain?" Philami had placed the yellow tea with the flakes from the stone in a clean water bottle. Now there was something about the stone's dust that made bitter things tolerable. So, Phil expected the bottle of liquid would not taste quite as bad as what John had to put up with.

"Ah, yaz all didentt nee ta go to a lot o holler for diz ol man whoz nary long fer dis worl."

"What would you do if you had a second chance at life. Is there anything you would do different?" The old man thought long and hard on the question. He got a far-away look in his eyes, then a sparkle came as he remembered his granddaughter. She was the only one who had paid him much mind as he grew more and more disabled.

"I'd go seez me granddaugtr, I'z would. She tell me can com lives wid her. She take good care of ol Popee she sade. Yez. Would pay her visiten. Show would. She liven in grand house in country. Gots cow and gardin wid fresh vegtbles, fruit. Happy days again I spect wid her." Phil had taken his box of ancient Chinese medicine with him. It was a beautifully handcrafted box made of cherry wood and inlayed with mother of pearl and precious stones. It had gold hinges and was bound in leather. He took out a glass tube with some ancient potion in it. Then he removed the cork and put a few drops on some comfrey leaves he had chewed in his mouth to form a poultice on the raw toes. These he wrapped with gauze. The old man was brought to tears by his kindness. Nobody had been so tender with his feet, ever. He was too emotional to respond. To think this man would come and minister to his needs was something he had never dreamed of. Phil now took the little bottle and handed it to the white-haired black man.

"Wishes do come true sometimes, Abel. I will make a deal with you. You would like to go live with your granddaughter Ruby, and she really would like that. I can see her now dressed up in her favorite pink dress with silk around the edges. And she has that strip of fir she likes to place around her neck just so she can feel the softness of it. She is thinking or you now, Able. Would you like to look in on her?"

"Mor den lif self," he responded as he took his grimy hands and wiped away the tears that were falling on his cheeks. Phil pulled out his pager device and punched in a code. I suppose we do not fully understand the technology of this, but we have a close second in the world. Just look at Facetime, or Zoom. You can see who you are talking to almost as if you were looking at them through a window. Ruby's face appeared and she was whispering as she looked out of the screen. Her words were. "I love you Popee. I am coming to see you soon. And nobody gonna keep me away from you no more." The old man smiled as he saw her smiling at him from the little window. He took the bottle of yellow liquid, drank it down in several swallows and lay back down on his filthy, lice ridden, flee contaminated cot. Several junk bugs better known as roly poly's tumbled on the ground.

CHAPTER 5

Chinese Proverb: It is not knowing that isdifficult,but the doing.

The next morning Abel woke up feeling better than he had in months. He looked down at his toes. The gauze was still wrapped around them. The exciting thing about it was the tingling sensation he felt. He wiggled first his big toes and then the others. They responded to his commands. It was raining outside. That was either good news or bad. Cold rains in the area were not fun but warm rains were a different matter. If this were a warm rain, he would take a shower. Sitting up on his cot he noticed a black plastic bag within reach of his hand. He pulled it to him and upon opening it found a fresh set of clothes. There was a new toothbrush with a small tube of paste. He also found a fresh bar of Irish Spring soap. Slowly he started pealing off his clothes. There were some areas where dead skin pealed off with them, they had been worn so long. He got up from the cot to complete the process. He was now stark naked. It was amazing that he could walk even to the point of gaining some feeling in his feet. Outside he chanced to look on the ground. There must have been close to a hundred dead rats laying all over the place. They were on the piles of junk and on the piles of crap he had tossed out his door. It was a strange thing to see. Twenty crows or so were gathered in the area having a feeding frenzy. There was one path that was cleared for him to walk in. He felt the rain, it was warm. He exited the shelter with the bar of soap and a washcloth and started scrubbing. "Lordy, Lordy bless my soul," he cried as the suds formed over his body. Layer by layer he worked his way down. The warm water from heaven washed it all away.

Back in his tent Philami smiled as he watched old Abel scrubbing himself in the rain. He was using what the ancient sages called the third eye. Back in Shangri-La some of the older lamas were totally blind so far as vision from their eyes was concerned but they could see more clearly with their third eye than with the physical ones. Indeed one of the ancient gods himself had a third eye and was known far and wide for it. His name was Erlang Shen. The third eye could see everything within a 360-degree circumference. Perhaps you are familiar with the term that a person has eyes in the back of their head? With the third eye-using the pineal gland-the ancients could see all around them. Even in martial arts this vision was fine tuned in some of the more advanced students who used it to gain an advantage over their rivals.

Another technique Philami had perfected was what you might call psychic energy generation, solidification or element manipulation. It took the better part of 20 years to master it. He had studied the secrets behind the flying carpets and magic ropes used in the middle east by some magicians from Bagdad. Movies like the 'Thief of Bagdad' and 'Aladdin' helped to popularize these unusual phenomena using actors with supposed superpower manipulation abilities. These he intertwined with similar phenomena used by the ancient Chinese masters. Their term for it was a bit different, something like psychic force-field generation. According to several renown Physicist, everything that ever was, is and will be exist eternally in the force field. So, in effect nothing is really lost. If a fire came and destroyed something you really liked it is possible to get it back if you know how. In this process you must get a clear enough visual image of an object-down to the minutest detail-in your mind then using the techniques named above, reconstruct it directly from the Force-Field using enhanced mental powers. People with this ability can appear to pull objects out of thin air. A strong mental picture had started to form in his mind. He fine-tuned his view, fashioned a three-dimensional mental image of it then reached out and drew it to himself. It was a beautiful Gibson guitar. He checked the manufacturer number. It was one of the first such models crafted. He estimated the current market value would be around fifty thousand US dollars even though the actual instrument had perished in a fire. Someone had had custom inlays embedded in the wood. Inside there was a signature of a famous country and western singer. Not knowing what else to do, the Oriental tuned into some forgotten talent hidden deep within his being. Beautiful music started coming from the instrument. In time he started to sing along.

In the opposite direction of old Abel's pad, about six camps over a middle-aged man heard the music and sat up in his sleeping bag. Back in his younger days he had been with a popular group. They had a good run of about ten years with several top singles. Then rap music had come to town and this older style lost steam with the producers. From doing gigs every week the demand for their band grew less and less. It had been an easy life back then. Money had never been a problem. All the band members had been hooked on drugs. While it lasted booze, drugs and women were as plentiful as the stars in the sky. Then they woke up one morning after an all-night bash with no more scheduled concerts. In a few weeks, the money they had between them was exhausted and the members went in different directions. It was over. Bobby as he had been called was forced to sell his beloved guitar to have housing and food for a year. When the money was exhausted, still addicted to drugs, he had found himself on the street. Now as the music entered his benumbed brain, he paused to remember. He had run into one of the band members just a few weeks ago.

Their sound was making a comeback. His buddies tried to get him to come back but fear of failure once again had caused him to hesitate. Then they were gone.

Phil saw all of this in his mind and was playing one of the very songs where Bobby had been the lead singer. He had it right down to the country twang used by the artist. It was still drizzling out. Bobby threw off the tarp and made his way slowly through the piles of trash to where the sound was coming from. Knowing of his coming the Oriental had deactivated the laser beams and sat just inside his tent with the flap open. Bobby came around another pile of trash and peered into the opening. He swore that was his old guitar in the hands of this Chinese man. At first, he was angry. Then as kept listening, the song did its switch at the end that required the listener to forgive his wayward woman. The singing stopped and from the opening in the tent he heard his name being called.

"Bobby, I know you are over their behind the burned-out car. Come over and play me a song or two. I must admit I am no singer. Would you be willing to come show me how it is done? I haven't sung a song like that in years." The guitar man exited from behind the old rig and pile of garbage before entering camp. He was surprised at how clean things were around this homeless man's tent. Most of the residents in dump city as some had termed it didn't give a rip what things looked like. Looking him directly in the eye the Oriental man continued speaking. "It looks like you are a bit groggy yet. Perhaps you are just waking up. I have a pot over the fire, I will make you a glass of hot tea. It will get your voice back in shape after your night's sleep." He proceeded to pour a cup of water over a bag containing some of the powdered yellow root. This would take Bobby's craving for drugs away for at least a couple of days while he shared some future options for his life. His back was turned away from the singer as he smiled thinking of the bright future he saw for this lost man.

Bobby was addicted to fentanyl. It was harder to recover from the cravings this resulted in because it affected a different part of the body than crack, cocaine, or acid. For this a few pinches of bitterroot needed to be added to the yellowroot. Bitterroot was harder to come by. It grew in semiarid portions of the country. In the spring a reddish colored stem would come up out of the ground and a pink flower would bloom later. Shortly after flowering, the entire plant shriveled up and died. Only a careful observer could find the plant then. The roots were almost like a bloodroot only orange in color. If you did guess right, one could always test the roots to be certain. Philami sprinkled a bit of powdered bitterroot in the cup. This would make it more effective. Phil bid the singer sit down before giving him the tea blend. He went and handed the guitar to him. Bobby took it eagerly in his hands. He looked it over real good. It was his long-lost guitar if it existed anywhere in reality. The name of the pawnshop owner was Bill. Bobby called him Billy. Bill had given him way less than what the instrument was worth. Remembering this Bobby started to talk.

"Billy ripped me off when I sold this to him. He should have given me another fifteen grand at least. How did you come by it? Billy's place got burned to the ground during the recent riots. He died in the fire according to eyewitnesses. I understood my guitar was lost in the fire but here it is in the flesh. There are only three more scratches in it from when I sold it. How could any homeless man afford this anyway? You could sell it and buy a small house." Phil pulled a bottle of furniture wax out of a satchel and handed it to the singer along with a soft cloth. Bob proceeded to remove the scratches along with two or three others he remembered were there before selling. Phil thought about the question for a couple of minutes than answered.

"The circumstances under which I came to own this are very unusual. You might not believe the story. So, are you going to try it out or what?" Bob's hands were shaking as he did a quick tune-up. When he tried to chord, his fingers had a hard time working the strings. They were out of practice and very stiff. He picked up the cup of tea and frowned as he took a sip. It was not a good taste or a bad one. Certainly, to like drinking this would have to be an acquired taste. Once he started though, he kept at it until the cup was drained.

"There is one weak string. It will go flat in about five measures," he complained as he struck it a few times and wiggled it to give it a bit of a wavering sound.

"I can't help you there, Bobby. That is the way it came into my hands." The country singer played a few notes and started to test his voice. It was also out of practice. He started humming and strumming the same song the Oriental had been singing. After a few minutes Phil noticed the shaking of his hands slow down. His fingers were less stiff and likewise his voice relaxed a bit. He did not need to strain to hit the high notes as before. Finally, he got the hang of it and gave a little concert. As he sang the gray clouds cleared and a bright sun came out. With the rain clearing the air, perhaps the moon tonight would be able to recharge the talisman the magician hid under his shirt. As the music swelled, the Chinaman sat down in his chair and started humming the harmony. Soon several of the local residents came by to listen.

After a little while one man brought a pail and started adding a beat. He found a couple of sticks and used them as if the pail were a snare drum. A more creative resident had taken an old spade and strung strings to it to make his own guitar of sorts and did fill in. A gal came by with a clarinet and added her sound. Every now and then some of the bystanders would join in singing. That was when by chance or predestination a local reporting agency, hearing the music coming from the homeless camp, stopped by and took some video of the odd mixture of musicians. It made the local news that very night. Off some three hundred miles away the rest of Bobby's band saw him leading out in this ragtag outfit. They would make one more attempt to try and convince him to come back. Phil knew there would need to be at least three more cups of tea to make the fix stick. He would need to hold onto the guitar for a little bit longer.

CHAPTER 6

Chinese Proverb: Give a man a fish and you feed him for a day. Teach a man to fish and you feed him for a lifetime.

And so, the days passed then the weeks. Each one brought a new character into contact with Philami. He seemed to have what was needed to better their life. Of course, being able to pull things out of thin air was a big plus. This ability was finetuned out in the raw world. Someone always needed something, and he could always get it. Bobby got back with his group. Ruby came and took her Grandfather out of his garbage pile. The engineer even was able to contact his sweetheart. They were not back together yet but at least they were talking. He had taken some of the money and purchased a cellphone. That helped with the transition a lot. Phil knew it was just a matter of time. The good news was he had not returned to the needle even once. About fifteen of the homeless people had left. Some found family members or old sweethearts. Others went back to some sort of civilized living. There were a few who went back to work at the same place they had been before something snapped and they were on the street. Philami wished he could help all of them but that was just not possible. Most of them did not want to be helped. They were right where they wanted to be. The ancient one wondered how the drugs kept flowing into the area even though most of the people didn't have any money. He didn't have long to wait. It was a chance happening although in the mainstream of time if one really knew the truth of the matter, nothing happened by chance. Someone somewhere high about it all had run the trillions of possibilities and worked out the one that best fit the moment.

The oriental man had taken his truck to a civilized part of town. There was a Chinese restaurant there and about this time he was craving food that was manufactured by his own hand. A drug deal was going down behind the building. He sent his third eye around the corner to the back to have a look. The van that had the drugs in it was in hiding. Word had come that a plain clothed officer had infiltered the supply chain. He was coming with a squad of at least fifteen agents to take possession of the stash. The handler's name was Samuel Weisman. He had several people under him. When their business was threatened like this, if they needed to dump a bunch of supply, they had a channel into three homeless populations in the area. For the homeless the profits were a lot less. That was a lot better than getting nothing for them, so contacts were made, and the van was emptied in record time. Just for show they left some miner drugs in there so the ones that made the bust could at least say they seized control of something. It would make it into the third page from the end of the newspaper. They were in it together for the most part anyway.

Philami pulled his eye back from the scene. He would ponder this situation for a few days, and do a little more exploratory research before formulating a solution. If he could manage to keep at least some of the drugs out of his camp, there would be a better chance of returning a good report once he got back to his bosses. Yes, I had to spill the beans sometime although I did not plan on doing it until the last chapter. Philami's little adventure in mine fields of the homeless was not a chance happenstance. There were powers high above him that had planned all this out for some greater good to the goals of their Order.

Phil knew he was there for a reason. They had not told him all the details, but he knew enough to go along with the plan where absolutely necessary and make his own choices where it not to change the outcome. He could choose his own ways and means to accomplish his part in the grand scheme of things.

There were some very powerful politicians that were making quite a bit of dough in this illegal drug operation. There were bribes passed around like candy on Halloween. People were paid to keep their mouth shut. He had been warned from his superiors to not muddy this water very much, but some things had changed in him after seeing the result of his work. There was a certain satisfaction is watching lives change before his eyes. For some it didn't take much change at all. He just needed to be there and point them in the right direction. For others, if they did manage to make improvements in their life choices, the results were not as speedy as one would like. Old habits are very hard to break and certain addictions even harder. But he would figure out how to cut off the supply line of these dastardly leaders who continued to get rich off the backs of the poor and helpless. Revenge would be sweet. Yet this revenge would need to be done in such a way that the powers that be, would be required to attribute the deviation from their goals to someone beside Philami. There must be no trail leading back to him. By the morning of the next day, he had a plan.

Three parties would each need to carry out their own portion of the strategy to make it work and cast blame on a criminal that had gone so long without being prosecuted that he considered himself above the law. He was about to be a fall guy for a planned departure from the Orders instructions. Phil already knew how to set him up. This would be a lot of fun! He would need to use psycho-ergokinesis techniques to alter reality. By hook or by crook he would gain access to Mitch's mind via subliminal, unimind techniques and this way influence him to do something that would result in an arrest with a penalty ending in several years behind bars. About this time however, and rather unexpectedly, Nathan arrived in camp. Let me share a little bit of his story with you.

From his earliest childhood Nathan was gifted with so many things. He was good looking with long blond hair and blue eyes. He was coordinated physically. If he decided to do a thing he always excelled. He was good at any sport you threw his way. He was quick to pick up new skills. Take learning a new job for instance. If he saw it once, he had it. A supervisor did not have to go over how to do something twice with him. He had another trait in those early years, Nate could look at a situation and pick the best rout to get through it. As he advanced in school, he found that the girls flocked to him. He was seldom without one or two on his arm. I would say most parents would have been proud of him during those early days. There was one girl that he did not seem to be able to manipulate though. Her name was Stephanie. She had this long, gorgeous, deep red hair. She was the top athlete among the girls at school. She could run like a deer. Turn her loose on a track meet and she would come home with all the prizes. It didn't matter if it was the hundred-yard dash or the standing broad jump. She was on top of it. All her teachers saw great potential in her. This was one student would make something of herself one day. Nathan wanted to be her friend in the worst way, but he could do nothing to persuade her to give him a second look, so he set a goal to win her to himself no matter how long it took. There was an old Chinese Proverb he heard one day that gave him hope. It went something like this: *Want a thing long enough and you don't.*

Tragedy struck these two young people about the same time. Nathan's dad died unexpectedly and Stephanie's mother up and left her dad for another man.

The fifteen-year-old was left with her dad. What does a man do with a fifteen-year-old daughter as independent as this one was? To make up for the loss of income, Nate's mother expanded her insurance business to another territory. This kept her away from home at least three days a week. When the two kids finally did talk one day, they shared their pain at the loss of a parent. Somehow it bonded them in a way nothing else could. Nathan finally had the girl of his dreams. She started hanging out at his house those nights his mom was gone. One day someone gave them a little pot to smoke. It seemed innocent enough but soon they were hooked. Then other drugs were introduced, and they begin to sink lower and lower. To make the situation more complicated, she got pregnant. What would they do now? Both dropped out of high school. Nate got a job with a roofing company and Steph took up hair dressing. She could take care of their little daughter Reanna that way and still help put food on the table. By this time, they had moved into their own place. Life settled down to the same old routine of booze and drugs along with work. The drugs were winning though. When he had a bad hangover, Nathan would not show up for work. This got him fired. He could always get a new job, however. Employers would snatch him up because when on the straight and narrow, he could do anything he put his mind to.

One day as he was in town, he met a young brunet, and you can begin to guess the rest of the story. He started spending more and more time with her and less and less time with his woman and child. To cope, unbeknown to Nate, Steph got ahold of some cocaine. She would do just about anything to get some, even steal. One day she got caught and the following night while Nathan was with Christel, the handler came and shot her in the back. She was left for dead. Somehow, she pulled through but never regained the use of her lower body.

This was more than the young father could deal with, so he left. It was then her mother decided to come back into her life to help with her granddaughter. Nathan became bipolar. If he took his medications, he did fine. Once off them for any length of time and he became impossible to live with. He started hearing voices in his head. At one point he said God had come to him and told him he would be the best rock star even better than Metallica. So, he sold some stuff and bought a guitar with an amp. He managed to get four friends to join his group. They practiced for days without ever getting even one gig. So that fell through. Another time when he got off his meds, he decided to read the Bible to get some answers. He read where Jesus stated if your eye offend you cut it out. Again he heard voices in his head telling him to do something outlandish. Christel was not his to have. Every time he saw her, he lusted. So. taking the passage literally, he tried to rip his right eye out of its socket. It resulted in total loss of vision on that side.

One day he put together a cocktail of 5 different drugs. Whatever little brain power was left quickly fled. Police found him running naked in the park, yelling at people to get out of his bathroom. So, he was sent off to a mental hospital. Over the next ten years or so he was in and out of the place multiple times. By this time, he wandered into the homeless camp, he had already been on the street for a decade. But now he had a steady stream of income. He read a Chinese Proverb: I suppose it would be close to being the opposite of the one printed above. It went something like this: *If you always give, you will always have.* This is where Nathan was that day he came barging into camp. He had just received his disability check and had cashed it out for fifteen, fifty-dollar bills. These he commenced to give out to every homeless person he met until they were all gone.

100

Philami scratched his head over this one. If the people here just lived on handouts, how could he ever hope to convince them to try and better their lives through effort and in many cases, just plain hard work. It became necessary to bend the rules a bit in the case of this new arrival.

CHAPTER 7

*Chinese Proverb: If heaven made someone,
earth, can find a use for them.*

It was time to win the homeless war in this area once and for all. What was it that caused a person to choose to be homeless in the first place? Obviously, homelessness is a choice or the entire world would be in the position of these pitiful examples of humanity. In Nathan's case, those first steps leading away from the path a normal person would take had set the course for the place he found himself in today. As the ancient sage reviewed his life during the night season, he was aware of several wrong choices this young man had taken. Were you to compare his potential as a child with a hundred others, these native abilities could have placed him among the top leaders in the world. Millions had done far more with a lot less. The question was how do you change a person that does not want to be changed? If they are content with nothing, how do you motivate them to desire anything? Desire after all is the flame that fuels all fires. He decided to break a carnal rule-that was to impose his will on the unsuspecting. There had to be several Chines proverbs against such an action, but times of great need called the need for powerful persuasion.

There was an ancient technique used by cult leaders that was kind of in the gray area of moral ethics. People with superior mental strength could force nearly anyone with less to do whatever they desired them to do. Powerful affirmations could be transferred to others during times when their mind could not consciously resist. The simplest name for this is mind control. He would dominate the minds of two parties needed to carry out his design and the second would bring it to the third. By the time this took place, Philami would be long gone thus deflecting the blame on the ones present. There were machines available that could broadcast subliminal messages over long distances. He had brought one from the great mountain to use only as a last resort. The homeless people in this area needed a leader and Nathan had the potential with a little help, of course to be a great motivator. He would lead them out, there would be an exodus from this camp and perhaps someone would take notice and research what happened, then taking this model, spread it to the hundreds of similar camps all over the United States and ultimately the world. The oriental plugged the machine into the power source and the vibrations went out to the entire area. Once the desired goal was reached, the machine would self-destruct and vanish into oblivion.

Phil formed a powerful affirmation and waited. As he monitored the mental state of this soon to be reformer, the moment arrived. Nathan had claimed to received commands from a higher source several times in his life and one came to him now out of thin air.

"Nathan, Nathan, you are to be my messenger. You have been chosen to bring great changes to this place. Know this one thing, what you start here, son, will be a flame that spreads around the world. Here is what you will do." The words struck his unconscious mind like a cyclone. The step-by-step guidelines had been planted in the unsuspecting mind of the recipient as surely as if he had come up with them himself. They were his own thoughts now. Step number one had been activated. Philami then formed a second affirmation for the criminal, Mitch who believed himself to be above all law and order. It would be through his influence and contacts that the transformation would be possible. Once the horror of his deed was publicized it would be too late and justice would be served. The ancient sage watched him like a cat would an unsuspecting bird. When the perfect moment arrived, a second message was sent. Mitch's mind was not powerful enough to resist.

"Mitch, no one has claimed ownership of the homeless camp at the south end of the city. All the property owners have abandoned their claim of any rights to the place. You can make millions and millions of dollars if you act now. I want you to contact your wealthy developer, George. Tell him you have a deal he cannot refuse." And so, the second party was activated. Specific instructions were beamed into his mind and etched there forever. He would activate the third with no further interference from the Oriental man who had just forced his will upon two unsuspecting individuals. It would take two weeks for the seed to sprout and grow. It had been planted in fertile soil and would surely reap a harvest. The question remained, would forcing the conscience of two people, even if it would accomplish great changes for good in this city, violate the power of choice each human had been endowed with at birth thus breaking some code of ethics? Humans had done this to others for thousands of years. It was normal in the course of government for all nations. Only one of the victims many choices had been forced into their consciousness. The hundreds of others that followed would be their own. Was it not ok then to do so since the result would be for the greater good of thousands and thousands of people and if he could read the future, eventually millions of people world-wide?

Things were about to change drastically in this valley of the lost and rejected. The ancient sage had completed his mission and then some. He had gone well beyond the call of duty and set into motion a course of action that would influence the whole. It was time to drive away now never to look back again. The old Ford truck slipped silently away during the still of the night. This one man from a different age of long ago, left a lot quieter than he had come. No one noticed as he headed out of town and dissolved into the evening mist. Back in camp the tent, shower, bathroom and firepit were all that remained. In the center of that square-perfectly carved out of trenches in the sand-were the words:

*HOMELESSNESS
IS A CHOICE*

HOMELESSNESS IS A CHOICE

EPILOGUE

Deep in the mountain of Karakal, Pangu, Jade Emperor, Nezha, Fuxi, Shennong, Zhurong, Guan Yu, Dou Mu Niang Niang, Zhongli and Erland Shen met (Lu, Dongbin) or Philami as he chose to name himself for this mission. He was one of the Eight Immortals known as the Ba Xian. These eight represented all the people in china-men, women, young, old rich, poor, noble and peasants. Each member of the group wielded a unique talisman that held the power to give life or vanquish evil. The gods had sent him on a mission to the United States of America. He was to enter into the lives of whoever he chose and bring back a report of his findings. Above all however, the Jade Emperor knew who he would choose to minister to so, it was not entirely by chance that he chose Philami to infiltrate a homeless camp in the center of the nation to see if the people there were open change. If the change started in the most deprived part of the nation, then who could determine that its purpose originated in China? It was a movement of stealth and strategy. Another of the Ba Xian would be sent on a follow-up mission to keep the momentum moving in the desired direction. Philami could now take a much needed, and well-deserved rest. It had taken a lot out of the old man. But he was back in the land of eternal youth. His physical being would be recharged and who knows? Perhaps he would venture back to check on those who he had influenced for good. It was not necessary for him to leave the mountain paradise, however. He could see them now, each in their new place of residence. What a change had occurred. Yet not one would ever remember or have even a hint of knowledge as to what happened to cause them to re-enter society. Jade Emperor ask the immortal a question.

"What have you determined the state of those you visited in America to be? Are they ready for an authoritative power to assert its influence on their culture?" The sage rubbed his chin as he pondered how to answer. In his dealings with the homeless, they had not desired to take themselves out of that environment they were in until a desire for a better life had been kindled within them. He had managed to point their focus not on their current situation but on what could be if the proper choices were made. Wrong choices had driven each of them there in the first place. They had been overwhelmed by the events that had come to them to such a point, they gave up hope of succeeding in the contest of life. It had been too competitive for their will and emotions to handle. Alcohol and drugs had been their salvation. These had filled the void and eased the pain that had taken root in their souls. Finally, he responded.

"I chose to work among the most deprived and hopeless citizens of their society. For the majority of Americans, these people of the street were cursed, they were the cast offs of their culture. They did not belong with the norm, so they were tossed away to rot and die in their own filthy surroundings. Nobody was ministering to them in anyway. They were worthless slaves of their own demise. I found that if desire is aroused again in their minds, if they could hope again, they can rise above their current circumstances and re-enter the stream of life as normal people. They had to be shown a vision of what they could become then helped along in their quest to attain that vision though. In answer to your question, I believe if the most pitiful and hopeless in that country can be influenced to once again be contributing members of society, those who have not fallen so low could also be motivated to change if given the proper vision."

It was the answer the council had been hoping for. America was ripe for a revolution if given the proper vision. All the pieces were in place. The ancient gods would once again assert their power over the masses, not only in China this time, but in the United States of America and then, worldwide. They dismissed the immortal, each heading off to their own separate quarters. The atmosphere within the mountain had not been so festive as it was now since these ancients had imposed their will over the Chinese empire millenniums ago.

What was the secret of his bounty? There are sources of power available that can be tapped into to bring about great change. Humanity as a whole does not live long enough to explore all the resources available to them in the vast universe. The secret of his bounty came from the abilities he acquired over centuries of self-sacrifice and study. He not only acquired the knowledge, he put it into practice once the techniques were perfected. The result, they formed a perfect weapon to cause changes to take place where no one else believed it could happen. There is another Chinese Proverb that we would do well to follow. If we can assimilate its secret and bring it to fruition, anything one sets their mind to can be accomplished. The only limitation we as mortals have is time. For most of us we only have a brief amount of it available in terms of the whole. For this immortal of the eight Ba Xian though, time was not a problem.

Chinese Proverb: If your mind is strong, all difficult things will be come easy; if your mind is weak, all easy things will become difficult.

WHAT WAS THE SECRET OF
HIS BOUNTY?